In memory of my father, Al Goldberg, and for Jesse~R.S.

To Spencer and his Dream Machines~K.H.

Orchard Books
95 Madison Avenue
New York, NY 10016

Manufactured in the United States of America
Printed by Barton Press, Inc.
Bound by Horowitz/Rae
Book design by Chris Hammill Paul

10   9   8   7   6   5   4   3   2   1

The text of this book is set in 17 point Centaur.
The illustrations are oils and acrylic.

Library of Congress Cataloging-in-Publication Data
    Schotter, Roni.
        Dreamland / by Roni Schotter ; illustrated by Kevin Hawkes.
            p.   cm.
        "A Melanie Kroupa book."
        Summary: As it gradually gets harder to make a living, Uncle
Gurney leaves his family and the tailoring business and heads West
with his nephew Theo's drawings to complete a mysterious project.
        ISBN 0-531-09508-8. — ISBN 0-531-08858-8 (lib. bdg.)
        [1. Tailors—Fiction. 2. Imagination—Fiction.]
    I. Hawkes, Kevin, ill. II. Title.
    PZ7.S3765Dr 1996
    [E]—dc20   95-23180

DREAMLAND

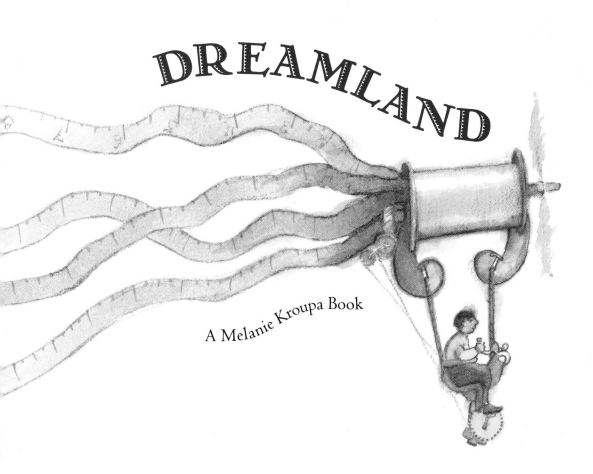

A Melanie Kroupa Book

Orchard Books
New York

DREAMLAND

by Roni Schotter

illustrated by Kevin Hawkes

Everyone always said I was just like Uncle Gurney. While Mama, Papa, and Aunt Ida worked long and late, turning jersey into jackets, damask into drapes, and tweed into trousers, Uncle Gurney snipped free-form flowers out of fabric.

"For you, Mrs. Levine," he'd say, presenting a customer with a bouquet of gingham gardenias. "For the little one," he'd wink, handing her son a herringbone horse.

When he should have been stitching straight, even stitches and cutting ever so carefully along dotted lines, Uncle Gurney's eyes strayed from his pattern while his lips talked of the day he would leave the family business behind and start a new life in the West. There, new ideas grew as fast and as easily as plums did on trees, and the air was warm and light and sweet with the scent of jasmine and oranges.

"Watch where you cut!" Aunt Ida always shouted, interrupting his daydreams. "You'll spoil the shirt!"

"There's more to life than measuring and cutting and keeping to a pattern," Uncle Gurney would say, proudly displaying his latest creation. "There's think and wonder and, best of all, imagine. Theo knows this, and so do I."

That's when Mama would shake her head and stare at the wall where she hung all my drawings. "I'm afraid my Theo and you are two of a kind. You both live in dreamland."

She was right. I *did* live in dreamland. When I should have been marking fabric with tailor's chalk, I was drawing my dream machines — chutes and slides and ladders and levers with names like The Spinning Machine and The Hoist and Spring.

"To what purpose?" Papa would grumble. "For what use?" he'd mumble, his mouth full of pins. "My brother and son have their heads in the clouds when their feet should be firm on the floor. They could use a little common sense."

"You never can tell," Mama would answer him. "Perhaps one day your brother and son will surprise you."

Time went on and life became harder. There were fewer and fewer customers and less and less work. One morning Uncle Gurney appeared, wearing his finest clothes. He was leaving—going West to seek his fortune. With money from Papa, a kiss from Mama, and tears from Aunt Ida, he was ready to depart.

"Good-bye, my Theo meo. I will miss you most of all. Promise you'll go on with your dream machines and when I have an address you'll send me some."

What could I say? I nodded, ran to the wall, ripped all my drawings down, and stuffed them into Uncle Gurney's hands. "Take them," I said, closing my eyes as tight as I could to keep myself from crying.

When I opened them . . . Gurney was gone.

Without Uncle Gurney, there was nothing to do but work harder than ever—in school, marking fabric, and, as I had promised, on my machines. One day a letter arrived from Uncle Gurney. Everyone dropped what they were doing, even Aunt Ida, who left Mr. De Mello, a valued customer, standing alone with only one trouser leg pinned on.

Uncle Gurney was fine and well and staying in a boardinghouse. He had great plans for a "project" he said, but he was keeping them secret for now. In his spare time, he'd been studying my dream machines and wanted to know how they worked. Could I send instructions? He sent kisses and hugs to everyone and to Papa the promise that one day he would pay back the money Papa had given him.

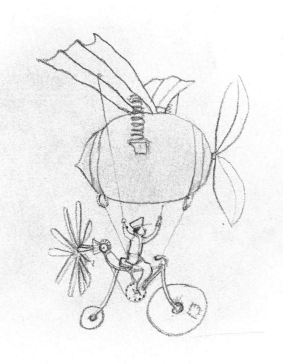

Over the next few days I wrote out instructions for my machines as best as I could remember—how The Spinning Machine worked, how to turn on The Hoist and Spring—and then, inspired by Uncle Gurney's letter, I designed my greatest dream machine ever. I called it Head in the Clouds in honor of Gurney. When it was finished, I hurried off to mail it and my instructions to him.

Every month brought another letter. Gurney and two new friends were working and living together in a house they had built in the "open air of an orange grove, making progress" on his mysterious "project." In one letter Gurney sent a packet of bulbs. "Plant these, water them, and in the spring, when they blossom, I will have news."

"He has friends," Papa said. "He's happy. But he hasn't changed. He still lives in dreamland. He could still use a little common sense."

Winter came, and there was even less work—more and
more time for dream machines. Soon the walls were covered
with new drawings. And every day I watched and watered
Uncle Gurney's bulbs, hoping for a hint of green. But week
after week, nothing grew.

"So? What did you expect?" Papa said. Mama, Aunt Ida,
and I glared at him.

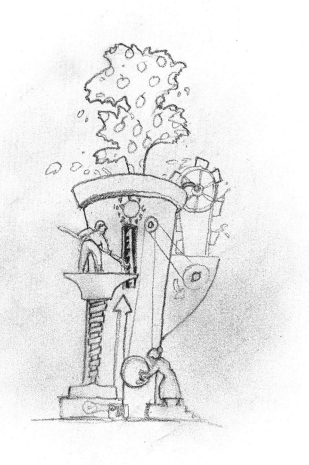

In March, except for an Easter dress for Mrs. Reilly and a Passover suit for Mr. Gold, we had no work at all. "Without work, what will we do?" Papa said over and over again. He and Mama and Aunt Ida were despondent, but I was full of hope. Uncle Gurney's bulbs had sprouted and were growing. One by one, buds appeared. Soon, I was sure, they would blossom and there'd be news.

On a cold morning in April, Gurney's buds opened—into lilies so large they looked like trumpets with something to say. That day too, an envelope arrived. I seized it and read the contents out loud:

"'Project nearly done. Everything in bloom here. Jasmine and oranges and lemons and figs! Imagine! Used the money I owe you to buy these.'" Taped to the letter were four bus tickets. "'Pack your bags. Meet you at the bus station. Gurney.'"

I turned to Papa, awaiting his answer. My heart pounded as fast as the needle on his sewing machine.

Papa sighed and shook his head. "Might as well," he said, finally. "No work, and we could use a holiday."

Day and night, night and day we traveled across the wide country on a bus, and then, finally, we were there and so was Gurney. When I saw him, all the tears I had kept so long inside came out.

"I have something to show all of you, especially you, Theo meo. Come," Gurney said, and he lifted me high up onto the back of a truck the color of the sky.

Off we drove through the windy Western air—in and out of fruit trees wearing bright spring jackets. In the warm fresh air even Papa couldn't help but smile—for the first time in months.

Bumping along in the back of the truck, Uncle Gurney told us about his new friend Miguel and how good a carpenter Miguel was and about his new friend Martin and what a good electrician Martin was and how hard he and his two friends had worked on their project, but how, even with the help of many others, there was still more to be done.

"Uncle Gurney," I said, unable to wait even a minute longer. "What *is* it? Please tell me! What is your project?"

"It's just around this bend," Uncle Gurney said, his eyes bright with excitement.

Then I saw it or maybe I dreamed it. . . . Moving, *spinning,* whirling, and sparkling with colored lights—my Spinning Machine, my Hoist and Spring, even my Head in the Clouds—all my dream machines, exactly as I had drawn them, but real now, and *running,* and larger than life.

"It's Dreamland," Uncle Gurney announced proudly, squeezing my hand so hard I knew I was awake, "and you, my Theo, designed it. We measured and cut, but it was you, Theo, who thought and imagined."

Papa's eyes were the size of winter coat buttons. "You have brought dreams to life," he said. "Amazing!"

Gurney's face blushed pink and broke out in dots like the dotted-swiss fabric Aunt Ida made dresses of. "But Dreamland is still not finished. It needs something more," Gurney said, smiling. "It needs my hardworking family with its good common sense to manage it. And it needs special suits for the men who will work here."

"Purple silk. With satin lapels." Aunt Ida sighed longingly.

"And dresses for the women."

"Sequined. With bugle beads," Mama breathed excitedly.

"And thick curtains for the ticket booths."

"Red velvet. With fringe," Papa whispered dreamily.

"And *many* new dream machines," Gurney said, looking at me.

"The Tailor's Miracle! With giant bobbins and huge pulleys and hoists," I said, reaching for my drawing pad.

And that is how we came to live in Dreamland.

And now, others come too — to take a spin on The Spinning Machine or a bounce on The Hoist and Spring, to escape their troubles, and for an hour or two, be filled with dreams and wonder.

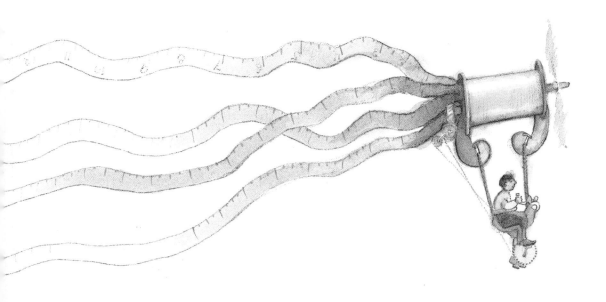